THE RAMSBOTTOM

Black Cats

The Ramsbottom Rumble • Georgia Byng
Calamity Kate • Terry Deary
Ghost Town • Terry Deary
The Custard Kid • Terry Deary
The Treasure of Crazy Horse • Terry Deary
Dear Ms • Joan Poulson
It's a Tough Life • Jeremy Strong
Big Iggy • Kaye Umansky

First paperback edition 2002
First published in hardback 2001 by
A & C Black (Publishers) Ltd
37 Soho Square, London W1D 3QZ

ISBN 0-7136-6173-9

A CIP catalogue for this book is available from the
British Library.

Printed and bound in Spain by G. Z. Printek, Bilbao.

THE RAMSBOTTOM RUMBLE

GEORGIA BYNG

ILLUSTRATED BY
HELEN FLOOK

A & C BLACK • LONDON

For my mum

Chapter One

A small, blue car drove at thirty miles an hour along the winding avenues of Bouring-on-Sea. Behind the wheel was Mrs Bugsby, a woman of thirty-five with flaming red hair, in an outfit that was halfway between army combat gear and frills – if you can imagine that.

In the car were her two sons. Tom, the elder (the brown-eyed one in the front), had hair which was brown and short, like a Doberman's. Like a fighting dog, he had scars on his face – one below his left eye and the other on his chin – and his two front teeth were chipped. He wore baggy trousers two sizes too big for him, with pockets all down the front and back, a huge tee shirt, and trainers that flapped open with their laces undone. By his feet were two footballs, a skateboard and a frisbee. Tom looked sulkily out of the window.

Dan, his younger brother, was sitting in the back seat looking fairly grumpy too. Dan had thick, shaggy hair that hung like a hairy curtain over his blue eyes. Protruding from beneath this fringe was a very large nose. He wore a tight, long-sleeved tee shirt with a butterfly on the front of it, a brown belt, and boots with a one-inch heel. On his lap was his denim jacket, onto which he was sewing a flower.

Suddenly, putting down his needlework Dan started to turn the window handle frantically.

'Are we nearly there? I think I'm going to be sick again, Mum,' he spluttered.

'Oh, Dan,' said his mother, hitting the kerb, 'just not in my handbag again, okay? I know it looks like a bucket but that's the design. Take some gulps of fresh air.'

'I feel sick at the idea of going to Granny's,' said Tom, sourly, from the front, ignoring his brother. 'For how long anyway, Mum? You never told us for how long.'

'For however long it takes for Aunt Saz to recover. One week? I don't know. She's going to be very sick after her plastic surgery.'

'Please stop talking about sick, or I really am going to throw up,' groaned Dan. For a moment, as the car rattled along, there was silence. Everyone was keen for the journey to end. Mrs Bugsby was late, Dan felt ill and Tom was restless. Since there was nothing to do, he started to play with words. 'Throw up, vomit, chunder, puke...'

'Tom, stop it. You're revolting,' said his mother, not really listening.

Tom continued. 'The best words are the onomatopoeic ones... like "puke", "puuuuuuke", it really sounds like it, doesn't it? Chunder's quite good too... "Chunnnnnnder". That really sounds like someone being sick. Whereas "vomit" is a useless word, doesn't sound like being sick at all.'

'Oh, stop it,' Dan managed to say. 'Or I'll be sick all over you. Mum – this is really bad. This road is

so bendy. Oh no! Ouuurgh!' Dan desperately poked his head out of the window, opened his mouth and stuck his tongue out.

'Lovely! Flies! Yum!' shouted Tom. Dan shut his mouth and swallowed hard; he was getting a grip on this sick feeling now and he wasn't going to let Tom distract him. His cheeks wobbled and his eyes watered as the wind hit his face. He'd been sick twice already and he felt green. What a way to start the holidays. It was bad enough as it was; because of his aunt going to hospital for her plastic surgery, Dan and Tom were missing summer club at The Polchester Theatre School. The school had at last realised how good Dan was at acting and this summer he'd been given one of the lead parts – a villain with a hooked nose. Like his aunt and his mother, Dan had the huge family nose. He liked his, but his aunt didn't like hers so she was going to have it made smaller by a plastic surgeon. In America. And so their mother was going to America, to keep their aunt company, and to see their dad too, who was there on business. Dan suspected that their aunt was going to have all sorts of other things fixed. Things made bigger and things made smaller. He wondered if they'd recognise her when she returned. Anyway, because of their aunt's nose, Dan was missing his big part in the play. As his eyes watered in the wind, he added a few real tears to the flow, and felt very sorry for himself. Then his mum slammed on the brakes and his head hit the window of the car. Tom, in the front seat, got a karate chop in the stomach as Mrs Bugsby protected him with her arm.

'Oooof!' said Tom, his eyes watering. 'That hurt, man. I've got nails in my tee shirt pocket.'

'I am not a man,' said Mrs Bugsby, 'and I've told you before, Tom, not to carry loose tools in your pockets. It's dangerous.' Mrs Bugsby shot through a red light.

Like his brother, Tom also took the opportunity of his eyes watering to shed a few tears. His tool kit... He'd been really looking forward to using that backstage at the summer theatre school. This year, he had been going to design, as well as build, the set. But now he was going to miss all that and stay at his gran's, in boring Bouring-on-Sea. How long for, was anyone's guess. The car came to another sudden halt and another karate chop in the stomach brought Tom to his senses.

They'd arrived. Tom and Dan peered out of the car. There was the pink façade that was the front of their gran's beauty parlour. There were the familiar pink letters above the shop, that read, 'Hannah's Heaven'.

'Phweeeh!' Dan breathed noisily. 'I'm so glad we're here.' Meanwhile Tom undid his safety belt and groaned morosely – he'd noticed that the shop next door had a newly-painted sign saying 'Pensioners' Paradise', but otherwise, the street looked exactly the same as last year; a quiet, Victorian street, full of dull shops for old people. Old people. Tom had never been to a place with more old people. This was good for trick or treating since the old people of Bouring-on-Sea usually had lots of sweets to give away, but it was not good for the summer holidays. Tom glanced at the winding street of shops and sighed self-pityingly once more. Then he caught his breath as he saw a woman, all in white, who looked like a character from a pantomime, stepping out of the beauty parlour.

'Haaalloooo,' she shrieked.

'Oh my giddy aunt,' said Tom, 'she's dyed her hair purple.'

'Looks stylish,' said Dan from the back, regarding her with his trained eye.

'Stylish if you like "Fluffy Poodle Style",' said Tom cynically.

'Well I do,' said Dan, just to annoy his brother.

'Hi, Mum,' said their mum, as she wound down the window. 'Look, I'm in a real rush. Dan was sick twice. I'm late for the plane. So I'll just drop them, if that's okay?'

'Fine, darling,' came their grandmother's sing-song reply, 'but drive safely won't you?' Their gran kissed her daughter, leaving a fat, purple lipstick mark on her forehead. 'And have a good trip. Give Saz and Dave my love.'

Dan and Tom climbed out of the car with their bags and belongings. There wasn't time for a long goodbye. So Mrs Bugsby kissed them both and scrunched their cheeks.

'Love you both, but I must fly. Really. Ha! Must fly.'

In a cloud of exhaust, Mrs Bugsby was gone. And the stay in Bouring had begun.

Gran waved as the blue car disappeared down the street, and then she descended upon her grandsons like a massive, six-foot paper doily. 'Oooooh la la!' she said, patting them both on their heads. 'Well haven't you grown! Golly gosh I can't tell which is the oldest any more.'

'I am,' said Tom sternly, wiping Gran's lipstick from his cheek.

'Of course you are, my daaarling, by a year. You must have been growing your clothes – gosh they're baggy – Tom, while Dan has been growing his bones and his hair! Goodness, Dan, your hair is so long, it's past your shoulders. I'll cut it for you, if you like.'

'No thanks, Gran,' said Dan, flicking his long hair out of his eyes. 'I like the look.'

'Of course you do, and so do I. It's just that you must find it difficult seeing anything. Now, what do you think of mine?'

At that moment, a lady with thick glasses tripped out of their gran's salon, only just saving herself from falling. 'Oh, Lady Horsehock! Mind yourself,' said their gran, hurrying to help her.

'Thank you so much, Hannah. That massage was wonderful, it's made me go all giddy,' said the tweedy Lady Horsehock in a grand accent. 'Pity I haven't got time for more, but I'll see you on Saturday, and I'll leave you to have fun with your lovely grandsons.' Lady Horsehock peered at Dan so that her powdered nose almost touched his. 'Oh, so one is a little granddaughter... I thought...'

'No, he's a boy. He's just got long hair, that's all.'

'Ah,' said Lady Horsehock, obviously disapproving. 'Well, see you on Saturday.'

At that point, a uniformed chauffeur put his arm under Lady Horsehock's elbow, and led her away.

'Poor Lady Horsehock. Blind as a bat,' said Gran as she turned to go inside. She didn't seem to notice the boys' long faces. 'Ooohh,' she said, bubbling with excitement. 'You are going to love my new decorations and we'll have so much fun.'

Tom's and Dan's hearts heaved as she pushed open the beauty parlour door and strange fragrances filled their nostrils. For them, 'Hannah's Heaven' was more like 'Hannah's Hell.'

Chapter Two

And so began the boys' holiday. Gran was delighted to be having her two grandsons to stay.

She led the boys through the beauty parlour reception room, with its clinical white and chrome chairs. On the walls were pictures of models with green sludge all over their faces, with captions like 'Find the New You,' and women in swimming costumes jumping up to the sky in a most unnatural way, as if they were trying to take off.

Gran removed her white overall to reveal a very frilly purple dress underneath.

'Gran, isn't that a kind of teenager's dress?' asked Tom, disapprovingly.

'Yes Tom, some people might say I'm mutton dressed as lamb, but I'm mutton having fun, that's all, if that's okay with you,' replied Gran with a twinkle in her eye. 'Because, recently, things have changed in my life. I'll tell you about it later.' With that, she stepped past the till desk to her apartment door, and pushed it open. Then she started up the stairs. Once or twice she nearly twisted her ankle in the very high shoes she was wearing.

'I like your shoes, Gran,' Dan commented. 'I've always liked platforms, but are you sure they're safe?'

'Not really,' said Gran, 'but you know what they say, "you've got to risk it for a biscuit."'

'What biscuit?' asked Dan, perplexed, but Gran didn't reply, as she was already through the door of her flat, heading for the kitchen to sort out tea.

Dan and Tom sat down awkwardly in Gran's green sitting-room. Gran liked to open her mind to other ways of living so each of her apartment rooms always had a different theme. The theme of the sitting-room this summer was 'Rainforest'. The table, which had been blue from last year's ocean theme, was now painted green, like a huge green leaf. Gran had even painted beetles on the leaf.

'Like the detail,' said Tom, genuinely impressed by Gran's workmanship.

'How about this, do you like this?' asked Gran disappearing behind a green, forest-pattern curtain.

While she was rummaging about, Tom and Dan examined their surroundings: the lampshade that had a fringe of felt leaves, and the armchairs that had huge, red felt flowers sewn onto them. Even the portrait of their big-nosed Grandpa, who had died five years ago, was decorated with jungle leaves. And in a corner of the room was an ultra-violet light, throwing its beams onto three exotic orange plants. Then all at once a frog croaked loudly. Tom and Dan looked about and under the chair to see where the noise was coming from. 'It's escaped, Gran,' Dan said nervously.

'No it hasn't,' said Gran, coming out from behind the curtain with a small green parrot on

Cheeky boy
Cheeky boy
Cheeky boy

her finger. 'He's right here. Do you like the soundtrack? It's "Tropical Sounds".'

'Great,' said Dan. 'I'm really glad it's not a real frog. I don't like frogs.'

'Cool parrot!' said Tom, forgetting his bad mood.

'Cool parrot, cool parrot,' said the parrot.

'Lovely, isn't he? He's six years old. Belonged to a man called Mr Twinch, who died.'

'Mr Twinch fell off his perch, Mr Twinch fell off his perch,' said the parrot merrily.

'He's ever such a cheeky boy. I call him Cheeky Boy,' said Gran.

'Cheeky boy, cheeky boy,' echoed the parrot.

'He's as good an impersonator as you,' Tom said to Dan, smiling, trying to make the peace.

'Now, I expect you two would like some cake. I got it from Marjorie's Tea House.' Gran fetched a plate with a cake on it from a sideboard. 'I'm sure people sometimes eat Victoria Sponge in the rainforest,' she said.

After tea, Tom and Dan took their cases to their room. Already, both were feeling more cheerful. Now they'd arrived, they'd both remembered that the best thing about Bouring-on-Sea was Gran. And Bouring wasn't that bad. After all, it did have the sea and the seafront. Besides, they both knew they couldn't be grumpy all week. And, it wasn't Gran's fault that their summer plans had been changed.

They discovered that their bedroom was now blue, that last year's ocean theme had moved there. There was an aquarium at one end of the room. 'Cool,' said Dan, going to look for the small green fish that he'd so enjoyed feeding before. But the fish had all gone. 'Where are the fish?' he asked, but before Gran answered, a huge reptilian creature flicked its tail, sending up sand.

'I'm afraid Donald ate them,' said Gran, biting her lip with embarrassment.

Donald shut his eyes lazily.

'Oh no!' said Dan mournfully.

'Bad!' said Tom. 'Cool! Is Donald a crocodile?'

'Yes, a baby one. But he has a big appetite. Arthur gave him to me. He isn't really a sea creature so he shouldn't really be in the ocean room. We'll just have to pretend he's a big fish.'

'A shark. A great white shark,' said Dan, who didn't like Donald the crocodile at all. 'And who's Arthur, Gran?'

Just then, a loud horn honked outside the bedroom window, and they all went over to look out. There on the street below was a very long, open-top, red sports car. Inside it, was a lean man in a blue blazer with brass buttons. The top of his head had a faint bald patch, but other than that his hair was black as boot polish, and neatly cut. He turned his face towards the front door.

He had a clipped moustache and was wearing dark glasses. Gran knocked on the window and waved. 'Yooo hoooo! Oh it's Arthur!' she said excitedly, looking at her watch and then rushing to the dressing-table to check her face in the mirror. 'Arthur's what's new in my life. Oooh, he's wonderful! I'll tell you about him later. But for now, I have to rush.' Like two pets whose owner was about to go out, Tom and Dan followed Gran into the tropical sitting-room where she whirled about like a purple tornado, gathering up her handbag, keys and purse, and putting purple lipstick on.

'Supper's in the fridge. It's macaroni cheese. Put it into the oven at one hundred and seventy degrees for half an hour. Look after yourselves, I'll be back at twelve. Any problems, this is my mobile.' She handed Tom a piece of paper with a number on it. 'Put yourselves to bed at nine, don't burn the place down, do brush your teeth, don't watch any 18 films and don't call any of those silly chat lines because they're very expensive, apart from anything else.' With that, their grandmother whisked her glittery blue coat off a chair and, in a cloud of perfume and powder, she left the apartment.

'Gran, slow down on the stairs, you don't want to break your ankle in those shoes!' Dan shouted out after her, worriedly. Tom, meanwhile, was chewing gum and looking out of the window, admiring the red sports car below. 'Wow!' he said as Dan joined him, 'I'd like a ride in that. That's an E-Type Jaguar... it's a classic car. Really expensive! Really fast.'

'I hope he's a good driver,' said Dan nervously, watching the man, Arthur, as he stepped out of the car to greet Gran. Arthur had taken off his blue blazer and was wearing a crisp white shirt underneath.

'Blimey, look at his cufflinks, they're huge,' said Tom.

Gran climbed into the front seat and started to put on a head scarf so that her hair wouldn't be blown about by the wind.

'Bet that E-Type goes fast,' said Tom. 'Just listen to the motor.'

'I wonder who he is,' said Dan.

Tom looked sideways at Dan. 'Well, obviously...' he said, raising a worldly eyebrow, '...obviously, he's her "fancy man".'

And the E-Type Jaguar sped away.

Chapter Three

At three a.m. in the morning, Dan woke up to hear Gran coming into the flat after her night out. He wondered how she'd ever get up for work the next day.

Gran woke up later than normal with puffy rings round her eyes that made her look like a toad. She put on her yellow kimono and her matching high-heeled slippers and came blearily into the kitchen where the boys were sitting at the counter. Both looked very at home. Tom was mending a broken tape-recorder. 'Morning, Gran,' he said. Dan was flicking through a TV magazine.  'Good date, Gran?' he asked, wondering how often Gran got up this late.

'Oh yes! And it's so nice to wake up with you

two here,' said Gran appreciatively. Then, making a pot of tea, she told her grandsons about her exciting night out.

'We had a lovely time. First, we went for a drive in Arthur's car. We drove to Beachy Point and watched the sunset and Arthur opened a bottle of champagne. He had glasses and everything. Then, after the sunset, we went for dinner at 'Les Trois Petites Pamplemousses', (that means, 'The Three Little Grapefruits'), which is the best restaurant in Bouring, and we had a delicious dinner! Caviar, the best wines and everything and chocolate towers for pudding, with a strawberry sauce. And then, then we went dancing. Arthur's a wonderful dancer! We did waltz, tango, foxtrot — you name it, Arthur can dance them all. But poor Arthur! He really had to dance his troubles away because, you know, earlier in the day, he had his wallet stolen. Would you believe it? All his cards and everything! Poor Arthur, he felt a bit lost without his wallet. But no point in crying over spilt milk, as they say.'

'So,' asked Tom, suspiciously, slowly putting down the tape-recorder. 'How did he pay for his dinner in the posh restaurant?'

'Oh, he didn't pay. I paid. Poor Arthur, it was very embarrassing for him.'

'More like very convenient,' said Tom, under his breath so that only Dan heard. Dan looked at

Tom questioningly, wondering what he meant.

'Anyway you two, I must stop nattering,' said Gran. 'I've got an appointment in five minutes, so I'd better get dressed. Will you let the lady in? I'll be down as soon as I can be.'

Tom and Dan willingly went downstairs to prepare Gran's treatment room for her first customer. The treatment room was pale green and pale pink, with silver and glass shelves. On the shelves were bottles of lotions and oils and creams, and on the walls were more pictures advertising beauty products. One picture was of a woman wrapped up in what looked like cling-film. 'She looks like she's ready to go in the fridge,' said Dan. Underneath her picture, it said, 'Try An Ionithermie Cellulite Super Detox Wrap Today'.

'Sounds like something on the menu of a take-away restaurant,' said Tom, as he turned on the radiator in the beauty parlour. 'And this Arthur, he sounds like a bit of a freeloader to me.'

'You're always so suspicious, Tom, as if everyone's out to get you,' said Dan, as he wheeled the trolley of nail varnishes out from a cupboard, realising now what Tom had meant upstairs. 'He probably did lose his wallet. You should be glad Gran's having some fun. She's been pretty lonely since Grandpa died.'

'Yeah,' said Tom, folding up some towels, 'but I have a feeling that having fun with Arthur is like having fun with...'

'With Donald the crocodile?' suggested Dan, 'No, I don't think so.'

'With a wolf in sheep's clothing,' said Tom. 'Gran's mutton dressed as lamb and he's a wolf in sheep's clothing. He's going to eat her up whole.'

'You're making it sound like Little Red Riding Hood,' said Dan, laying a towel on the treatment couch. 'And you've got it all wrong. The problem isn't Arthur. The problem is Gran. Look at the time! She's late. She used to be such a stickler for time. It's not good if she's late for customers. Her business has taken years to build up but she'll lose her regulars if she's late for them.'

A ring on the front door bell announced the arrival of Gran's first customer. She was a thin, wrinkled woman in a black-and-white chequered coat and a beret, with stick-like legs. As she delicately stepped through the entrance, a tiny Chihuahua hopped in with her. 'Come on Poochie,' she said to the miniature dog.

Dan looked her up in the appointment book, and put on his best receptionist voice. 'Good morning Miss Lichens. Hannah will be down in a minute. Can we get you a cup of anything?'

'Oh yes please,' said the skinny Miss Lichens, with her Chihuahua now on her lap, 'I'll have a cup of coffee please.'

Tom went to the small kitchen behind the

waiting room, to make Miss Lichens a cup of coffee. He wasn't quite sure how to make coffee, but he'd have a go at anything, so he put five spoonfuls of granules into the cup, until the coffee looked nice and black.

By the time Hannah came downstairs, carrying

Cheeky Boy in his cage, Miss Lichens had drunk three cups of Tom's ultra-strong coffee. With all the caffeine inside her she was talking very, very fast. 'Oh, hello, Hannah, lovely to see you – oh and Cheeky Boy too – and your grandsons have looked after me so well – I like your new hair, purple is it? Maybe I should go for purple too – or maybe on second thoughts I'll go for my normal pink rinse,' she said at a hundred miles an hour.

Cheeky Boy cocked his head to one side as she spoke. He'd never heard any one talk so fast and he wondered whether he might be able to copy Miss Lichens. Then he decided against it and simply said 'Pink rinse, pink rinse.'

As Miss Lichens chattered away, Gran led her and her Chihuahua into the treatment room.

'Do you think Gran does the Chihuahua's hair too?' asked Dan.

'Paints his toenails an' all,' said Tom.

'Really?'

Tom picked up his frisbee. 'Dan, you're so gullible. Fancy chucking this about a bit?'

'Okay,' agreed Dan, and they stepped outside into the sunny street.

By afternoon, Gran felt so tired that she had to cancel the rest of the day's appointments. 'I'm so sorry Mrs Pembroke,' she said, stretched out on her rainforest sofa, in her yellow kimono, 'It's just that I think I'm coming down with something.'

'Yes, Arthur-itis,' said Tom, quietly. Gran yawned and put the phone down.

'You ought to rest,' said Dan, worried about how tired Gran was. 'You look ill. Late nights aren't good at your age.'

'You're right, Dan. I'm no spring chicken. So here's a couple of quid for chips. Go down to the seafront and muck about. I'll see you later.'

As Gran went to her bedroom, Dan shook his head, and flicked his long hair out of his eyes. 'This is bad news, Tom. Business is going to slip if Gran doesn't get her sleep.'

'Oh, stop worrying,' said Tom, as he examined the tools in Gran's manicure kit.

They heard a shriek of laughter from next door. Gran was obviously having a quick chat with Arthur on the other phone, before her rest. Tom's lip curled.

Tom and Dan left the Beauty Parlour and set off for Bouring seafront. They soon forgot about Gran and Arthur, as there was so much to do by the sea. First, they skimmed stones, which was fun, until Dan, who wasn't a good aim, hit an old man hard on the ankle. Dan felt very guilty and

rushed up to the man to apologise.

'Don't worry girlie,' the old man replied, 'It's good to see pretty girlies skimming stones. You just need to practise more, like your brother.' Dan smiled lamely as the man hobbled off, while Tom laughed, throwing a stone that skipped merrily across the water seven times. 'Okay girlie,' he teased Dan, 'Let's do some construction work.'

After building sandcastles, Tom and Dan went to the amusement arcade, where they spent most of their fish and chip money on the slot machines. Dan was embarrassed to be with Tom, who shook the penny-fall machines, trying to dislodge the money there. Later, it was Tom's turn to be embarrassed by Dan, when he joined in with a busker on the street, singing 'Oh I do like to be beside the seaside'. After this, it was quits on the embarrassment front, so the boys bought ice creams and strolled back to Gran's.

Chapter Four

When Tom and Dan got home it was five o'clock and the red E-Type was parked outside.

'Uuurgh, Mr Smoothie's here,' said Tom.

Sure enough, inside upstairs, Arthur was sitting in Gran's tropical sitting room, smoking a cigarette. Tonight he was wearing pointed plaited-leather shoes, black, slinky trousers, a black shirt, a black suede bomber-jacket and a yellow silk cravat around his neck. It was a waspy look. Arthur's black hair was slicked back and his moustache was well combed. He smiled as the boys entered, revealing a crooked row of teeth. Dan thought he looked all right, but Tom didn't like the way Arthur was relaxing on the sofa, as if he was at home. He felt like grabbing Arthur by the collar and throwing him out.

Gran, in a tight pink dress, was blushing. 'Ooh, boys, I'm so glad you're here. Meet Arthur. Arthur, this is Tom and this is Dan.' Arthur uncrossed his bony legs, rose from his chair and held out his hand out for a handshake. He wore a gold signet ring on his hairy little finger.

'Pleasure to meet you,' he said, wrinkling his nose and winking. Dan and Tom both shook his hand which was limp and soft.

'Like your car,' said Tom. 'Can we have a ride?'

A flicker of unwillingness crossed Arthur's face before he controlled himself and smiled.

'Oh, do give them a spin, Arthur,' said Gran. 'They'd love it and it would make up for me sleeping all afternoon.'

'Give 'em a spin, give 'em a spin,' said Cheeky Boy, and before Arthur could make any excuses, he'd been talked into giving Tom and Dan a ride. Dan was nervous of the car, so he sat in the back. 'Can we have the roof down, Arthur?' said Tom.

'Oh, go on, Arthur, put the roof down,' said Gran. Arthur was beginning to wish he hadn't dropped round. He heaved the roof back and then slid into the black leather driving seat.

'Where to?' he asked as enthusiastically as he could.

'The waterfront,' said Tom.

Gran waved them goodbye, and soon they were speeding along the avenues near Gran's house. Arthur wore his yellow driving gloves, the E-Type's engine roared, and its long red bonnet swung round in front of them as Arthur accelerated around corners.

'Oooerrrgh, I feel sick,' shouted Dan from the back, his hair flapping in the wind. Arthur put his foot on the brake immediately and the car screeched to a halt. Like a jack-in-the-box, he bounced out of the car, pulling Dan out in the same movement.

'Not in my car you don't,' he said.

'He's not really going to be sick,' said Tom.

'Yes I am,' said Dan.

Arthur looked concerned. 'I tell you what, boys, why don't we get out here?' Arthur gestured to the roadside café where they'd stopped. 'We can have a cup of tea and a breath of air, while Sam recovers.'

'I'm Dan,' said Dan.

'Yes, well, while you recover.'

So they all went into the café where there were rows of red formica tables with red padded chairs along their sides. They sat down at a table by the window and the sun poured through. In the bright light, Dan was sure that he could see make-up on Arthur's wrinkly face. 'What would you like?' asked Arthur. Tom and Dan studied the menu.

'A chocolate milkshake, please,' asked Tom. 'If that's okay.'

'A glass of water, please,' said Dan still feeling green.

Arthur ordered their drinks and a coffee for himself.

'So,' he said, in what he thought was a pally I'm-your-new-buddy kind of voice, 'So how are you two enjoying your stay in Bouring-on-Sea?'

'It's fine,' said Tom. 'Gran's got two new pets...'

'Ah, yes,' said Arthur, 'Cheeky Boy and

Donald. I like Donald, he takes me back to the time I was in Africa.'

'Why were you in Africa?' asked Tom.

'Well I was employed, er – actually this is rather a tricky subject...' said Arthur, his sentence coming to a strange, grinding halt. Arthur looked the boys up and down, and drew his chair up closer to the table. 'I suppose I can trust you. After all, you are Hannah's grandsons.' Tom and Dan looked perplexed.

'Trust us with what?' asked Tom.

'With what I'm about to tell you.' Arthur looked about the café as if checking that the coast was clear. Then he said quietly, 'Can you boys keep a secret?'

'Yes,' they both said, wondering why Arthur had gone so quiet and conspiratorial all of a sudden.

Arthur gave them both one more look as if sizing them up. Then his left eyebrow went up and down, and he told them his secret. 'I... worked – well, I still do work – for British Intelligence,' he said.

'What's that?' asked Dan. Tom crossed his arms and leant back in his chair. He smelt a rat.

'British Intelligence,' said Arthur, 'or MI6, is the organisation that trains and uses spies, for Britain, all round the world.'

'What? So you're a spy?' said Tom, a little too

loudly for Arthur's liking. 'Sorry,' said Tom, 'it's just that I've never met a spy before. No wonder Gran likes you.'

Arthur chuckled. 'Well, I hope she likes me for more than just my profession.'

'A spy for MI6,' repeated Tom, slowly. 'Fancy that.' Tom was always suspicious of people telling lies; there were a couple of boys at school who told lies all the time.

Arthur looked at his coffee cup. 'Yes, MI6. That mysterious organisation. But you boys must keep that information to yourselves. If it got into the wrong hands, it would be curtains for me.'

'So,' asked Dan, amazed, 'did you have to learn all that James Bond stuff, like how to use guns, and how to defend yourself?'

'Yes,' said Arthur, in what seemed to Tom like his best James Bond impersonation. 'Do you boys know any martial arts?'

'No,' said Tom and Dan in unison.

'Well,' said Arthur, 'I'm trained in aikido, judo, kung-fu, karate, kick-boxing. I'm a black belt in all the Eastern martial arts.'

'Cool,' said Dan. 'Do you use all the styles all at once, when you fight?'

'Yes, and of course I have to use a gun. When I don't have a gun, I have to disarm an opponent, or six opponents. That's when it gets crazy. I've floored fifteen men single-handedly. It

EEEIIAAHH

amazes me sometimes to think how I've won against the odds.'

'Have you killed anyone?' asked Dan, in awe.

'Yes. In the wilds of Borneo once, I killed 26 men in half an hour. I don't like to do it, but sometimes it's necessary. It's a job, and I'm trained to shoot to kill.'

'You must have travelled all over the world,' said Dan, very impressed.

'I have, and I've met some of the most important people in the world, not always in the nicest of circumstances.'

'So what are you doing in Bouring-on-Sea?' asked Tom, bluntly.

'Lying low for a bit,' said Arthur. 'Now look you two, if ever you see me in Bouring with someone, a man or a woman, you mustn't come up and say hello. You must pretend not to know me, and I won't know you. Got it?'

Both the boys nodded.

On the way back in the car, Dan asked if the car had any special abilities, like James Bond's did. 'Oh no,' said Arthur, 'this car's a lamb. My working car is kept at Head Office in London.'

By the time they'd got back to Gran's, Tom and Dan could see why Gran admired Arthur so much. But the difference between them was, Dan believed every word he'd said, whilst Tom thought Arthur was a lying snake.

Gran was waiting on the beauty parlour doorstep, all dressed up with flowers in her hair.

'Arthur and I are going out now, boys. I'll be back later. Wake me up in the morning would you? And behave yourselves.'

'Goodbye Tom and Sam,' said Arthur, laddishly winking at the boys. With that he put on his yellow driving gloves, helped Gran into the E-Type and slid once more into the driving seat. The car purred its way down the road and was gone.

'Wow, a spy,' said Dan, tying his denim jacket round his waist. 'Maybe I should go for the James Bond look.'

'The James Bond Girl look,' said Tom ruffling Dan's hair. 'Dan, you ought to get your fringe cut. It's making you blind. Can't you see? The guy's a fraud.'

'Well, actually Tom, I don't think he is. He

wouldn't make all that stuff up. You're so cynical and out for a fight. You're suspicious of everyone. If a two-year-old offered you a sweet you'd think it had poison in it.'

'I'm just realistic,' said Tom. 'And if that Arthur is for real, I'll eat my...'

'Baseball cap?' suggested Dan.

'My skateboard,' said Tom.

Chapter Five

On Saturday, Gran did not wake up for breakfast, so Dan made her a cup of tea and took it to her bedroom. He knocked at her bedroom door, then went in. The theme of this room was Ancient Japan, so the walls were decorated with pink blossom trees and there were rush mats on the floor.

To Dan's disappointment, the room was quiet. It seemed that Gran wasn't there. The bed was made. Its black satin cover was smoothed down and its golden cushions were plumped up.

'Gran!' called Dan, thinking that she might be behind a screen.

'Nice to see you,' said Gran in a very croaky morning voice.

'Oh, Gran,' said Dan with relief, 'I thought you weren't here, I've got you a cup of tea.'

'Clever boy,' said Gran.

'Well, not really, I've been making tea for ages. I can make pancakes too.'

'Clever boy!'

'If you say so,' said Dan.

'I like nuts, nuts and berries,' said Gran.

'Really? For breakfast? If you tell me where you keep them, I'll get you some.'

'Cheeky boy,' said the voice, 'cheeky boy.'

Suddenly Dan realised who it was behind the screen. Sure enough, when he walked behind it there was Cheeky Boy balancing on a bar in his cage, with his head to one side.

'Big nose, big nose,' he squawked.

'Thank you,' said Dan.

Cheeky Boy was clever. Dan took him out of the oriental bedroom, and into the tropical sitting-room. 'Tom,' he said seriously, 'Gran's not in.'

'Well,' said Tom, 'we're not her parents. She's allowed to stay out.'

'No,' said Dan, 'what I'm worried about are her appointments this morning. The first one's usually at 9.30 and it's 8.40 now. What if she doesn't get back?'

'Oh, she'll be back,' said Tom nonchalantly sipping a hot chocolate. 'Double O Six will drop her off.'

But by 9.15, Gran had not returned. Tom and Dan prepared her rooms, turning on the lights and the fountain in the waiting room. Dan looked in the appointments book. '9.30,' it said, 'Lady Horsehock.'

37

'Crumbs,' said Dan. 'Lady Horsehock's one of Gran's best customers, and she's booked in for the day. I mean, I like Gran going out but she's going to lose customers if she doesn't turn up for them.'

'She'll be here,' said Tom, a little less sure this time.

Lady Horsehock's Bentley drew up outside the beauty parlour at 9.29. As the wizened old lady bid her chauffeur goodbye, Dan and Tom prepared to greet her.

'Morning,' said Tom. 'Cup of tea or coffee Lady Horsehock? Our gran will be ready soon.'

'Oh, yes, tea please,' said the grand old lady, taking off her cream silk coat. 'Would you please hang this up for me? I'd do it myself, but my eyesight is so bad I can hardly see you.' Dan took her coat, which smelt of horses.

By 9.40, Lady Horsehock was on her second cup of tea and was beginning to look impatient. Dan pulled Tom into the small kitchen. 'Tom, this is bad.'

'I know, but what can we do?'

'I'll tell you what. We're going to pretend to be Gran,' said Dan.

'We're going to what? Are you mad? Gran's enormous and you and me are tiny. Lady Horsehock's not that blind.'

'I wasn't thinking of us being our normal sizes,' whispered Dan. 'I'll get on your shoulders and I'll put on Gran's white overall. The bottom part of it will cover you and if you take off your trousers, your ankles and shoes will look like Gran's.'

'Dan, have you gone completely stark raving mad?' spluttered Tom.

'Listen, once we're in the treatment room, we can make her shut her eyes, and then I'll get off your shoulders. I've watched Gran enough to know how to do lots of the treatments. And you know I can imitate Gran's voice perfectly. Trust me.'

'Trust you? Trust a lunatic like you?'

'Tom,' said Dan in an unusual low growl, grabbing his brother's sweatshirt collar and giving it a tug, 'Do you want Gran to lose customers? Do you want her business to fall apart?'

'N...nope,' said Tom.

'Well then, do as I say, and come upstairs quickly.'

Three minutes later, Dan and Tom came out of Gran's apartment door, Dan on Tom's shoulders. Dan had put a white scarf on, to cover his hair, Gran's big spectacles – the spectacles she liked to work in – and a white overall that covered Tom.

Lady Horsehock's eyesight was very bad. It was as if a sheet of ice was always hanging in front of her face, even with her glasses on. And so, when Tom and Dan approached, with Dan saying in his best Granny Hannah voice, 'Ah, Lady Horsehock, I'm so sorry to be late,' Lady Horsehock didn't suspect for a moment that this was not the real Hannah.

'Hannah, don't worry. Your grandsons have been looking after me marvellously.'

'Well, I'm glad,' said Dan, stepping towards the treatment rooms, wobbling slightly. 'They've gone off to play football now, so shall we go in?'

'Yes, let's get started. It's lovely to have a whole day of treatments,' said Lady Horsehock feeling her way along the wall to a screen, behind which she disappeared to change into a towelling dressing-gown. Tom reached out and turned the lights down low. 'I've been reading about relaxation,' said Dan, in Gran's voice. 'It's best to have lights dimmed during treatments.'

'Oh yes, I agree,' said Lady Horsehock, appearing in a pink towelling dressing-gown. 'Now that's the treatment couch isn't it?' she said, squinting at the furniture in front of her and then sitting.

'Er, no, you've sat on a cupboard,' said Dan, directing Lady Horsehock to the treatment couch, and he added, 'I noticed that your eyes look very tired. I think it would be a good idea if you put these cool cucumber compacts on your eyes. Then those bags under your eyes will disappear by the end of the day.'

'Marvellous,' said Lady Horsehock, settling back on the couch and taking off her spectacles. Tom struggled as he carried Dan to the cucumber compact tray and then back again to Lady Horsehock. Tom's strength was beginning to give way; Dan was just as heavy as he was. As Dan leant over to place the cucumber compacts on Lady Horsehock's eyes, Tom found it difficult to keep upright. And then, for a horrible moment, he began to topple forwards. As he fell forwards, he just managed to avoid falling on the frail Lady Horsehock. Tom stumbled forwards and Dan hit the mirror with his body, knocking some bottles onto the floor. Tom tried not to laugh. (He often laughed in tense situations).

'Are you all right, Hannah?' said Lady Horsehock, concerned and beginning to sit up.

'Yes, yes, don't get up, I tripped over a towel that's all,' said Dan pushing himself onto Tom's shoulders again.

Tom stepped towards the old

lady for a second attempt.

At last, Lady Horsehock was safely under cucumber compacts, and Dan slid quietly off Tom's shoulders. Tom rubbed his shoulders, while Dan turned on Gran's 'relaxing' music, which was the sound of whales singing to each other against a background of harps playing. 'Now, Lady Horsehock,' said Dan. 'You really mustn't remove those cucumber eye compacts or the minerals won't get into your skin.'

'Which minerals are those?' asked Lady Horsehock, wiggling her long white toes.

'Erm, mineral water sort of minerals,' guessed Dan.

'Ah, very interesting.'

'So,' said Dan, 'What shall we start with? Foot massage and toenail manicure?'

'Yes please, that would be lovely.'

Tom thrust a handwritten note in front of Dan:

> You LUNATIC. What are you going to do if Gran comes back?

Dan read the note and remarked to Lady Horsehock, 'I like your pink nail varnish.' Then he shrugged his shoulders at Tom, and started to fill a foot-soak bowl with bubbly water.

Chapter Six

So began Lady Horsehock's treatment day. Dan and Tom took it in turns to massage her bony old feet, which luckily weren't smelly at all. Then Tom set to work, clipping and filing her claw-like toenails. Tom was used to handling tools so he thought this was the best job for him, but in his confidence, he forgot Lady Horsehock was a human being and not a piece of cardboard or wood. He accidentally clipped her skin. Lady Horsehock yelped in pain.

'I'm so sorry,' said Dan, glaring at Tom. 'My hand slipped. That shan't happen again.' Dan grabbed the tools from Tom and pushed him aside.

After her feet had been creamed and polished and her nails repainted, Dan and Tom gave Lady Horsehock a 'facial'. This involved using every sort of cream that they could find on Gran's shelf with a label that said 'face cream'. Tom chose the creams and passed them to Dan, along with cotton wool to wipe the creams off. Then Dan put a mud face mask on the old lady and said, 'You just relax with that on and I'll be back in ten minutes... don't get up now.'

With that, he and Tom went out of the room.

'Crumbs,' whispered Dan. 'That was hard work, but so far so good. The trouble is, look, the diary says she's booked in to have her eyebrows plucked as well.'

'And her hair dyed,' whispered Tom.

'And a massage. Oh my giddy aunt. I am not giving her a massage,' said Dan with wide eyes.

'You'll have to make some excuse then,' said Tom, 'because I'm not doing that either. That would be too embarrassing. Look, you do her eyebrows, and I'll read the instructions on the dye packet. It'll be a cinch. Just like mixing paint.'

So Tom and Dan went back in. Dan removed the mud mask with water and cotton wool and Tom passed him the tweezers. His hand was a bit shaky to start with but soon Dan was plucking away happily. By the end of the plucking, Lady Horsehock didn't have much eyebrow left, but they looked like posh old lady's eyebrows, or so Dan thought.

Tom, meanwhile was mixing hair dye. He nudged Dan and pointed to the mixture in the pot. 'Black or brown hair this month?' asked Dan.

'The normal colour,' said Lady Horsehock, and ten minutes later she had a head covered in brown paste. After another ten minutes, Dan rinsed this off in Granny Hannah's movable sink, and then he began to blow-dry her hair. 'No rollers this week?' she asked.

'Er, no, no curlers; I thought we'd go for the blow-dried look,' said Dan.

The uncurlered look was fairly wild. And, all in

all, by the end of the blow-drying, Tom thought that Lady Horsehock had definitely looked better before she came in. Her hair was an orangey colour, since Tom had mixed the dye incorrectly, and she had a stain of dye on her skin around the top of her forehead. Also, her eyebrows were – well, they were gone, really.

Dan climbed back onto Tom's shoulders, and they put the overall on.

'Lady Horsehock, I'm afraid that's it for now. I won't be able to do the body massage today as I've hurt my back.'

'Oh Hannah,' said Lady Horsehock, taking off her eye patches. 'I'm so sorry to hear it. I thought you looked a bit crooked.'

While Lady Horsehock went behind the screen to change back into her clothes, Dan made conversation with her, as he'd heard Gran doing.

'So, Lady Horsehock, have you got a nice weekend planned?'

'Well actually, Hannah, to let you in on a little secret,' came Lady Horsehock's excited reply, 'I've got a date! I've met a lovely chap, who, would you believe it, is a... well actually, I'm not supposed to tell anyone, as his profession is top secret, but I know I can trust you. He's a spy!'

'What's his name?' asked Dan, amazed by the coincidence.

'He's called Arthur,' said Lady Horsehock, 'and

he drives a very fast car. Thank you so much for making me look my best for him. We're having dinner this evening.' Lady Horsehock came out from behind the screen. She looked a sight, with wild, orange hair, a dyed forehead and no eyebrows.

'Yes, well you look lovely,' said Dan gulping.

Tom was practically suffocating by the time Lady Horsehock left. 'Ooof,' he grunted, as Dan got off his shoulders. 'Next time I'm going on top.'

'I hope there won't be a next time,' groaned Dan, sitting down with his head in his hands.

Chapter Seven

Gran didn't return until five o'clock on Saturday afternoon. 'Oh, I'm so exhausted,' she said, putting her bags down on the kitchen sideboard with a satisfied sigh, and giving Tom and Dan a kiss. 'Sorry not to be back earlier, but I was having so much fun.' Dan put the kettle on, glad that she was back; he'd been worried.

'What did you do, Gran?' asked Tom, who was lying on the sofa, tired from an afternoon's skateboarding. He was doodling and trying to draw a cartoon of Arthur.

'Just about everything,' sighed Gran, with a faraway look in her eyes. 'We went to the edge of the world and back. We drove to London and we stayed in a very fancy hotel, and we went on the London Eye, and we went to a show, and a casino – would you believe it? And we ate lovely food and I bought a new hat and Arthur got one too, because next week we're going to the races.'

'Has Arthur found his wallet, then, or had his stolen cards replaced?' asked Tom, drawing a patch over the eye of his cartoon of Arthur, and a parrot on his shoulder.

'Oh no,' said Gran. 'You see, it's terrible having your wallet stolen because it takes about ten days to have all the cards replaced. Poor Arthur. He says he feels like a child with me paying for everything.'

'You paid for everything again?'

'Well yes, Tom darling. What could we do otherwise?'

'Poor Arthur,' said Tom, but Hannah didn't detect the sarcasm in his voice.

'And what's he doing tonight?'

'Well, he's on a mission,' said Gran, innocently, slumping into an armchair. 'I must say, it's very inconvenient working for the secret service. They use Arthur any time they like. He has to drop everything he's doing and go and do his duty.'

'Poor Arthur,' said Tom again, thinking of Arthur in a restaurant with Lady Horsehock.

Dan came and sat on the arm of Gran's chair. He soon found out that she had no memory of missing any appointment that morning, so he ran downstairs and rubbed out Lady Horsehock's name in the diary. He thought Gran might be furious if she found out what they'd done.

Gran, meanwhile, oblivious to the plotting and scheming around her, spent Saturday evening cooking and singing love songs to herself. Cheeky Boy was very pleased to have her back and whistled along with her.

Tom and Dan disappeared off to their room for a meeting. They fed the baby crocodile pieces of bacon as they talked.

'Let's rename him Arthur,' said Tom looking at the baby crocodile. 'Arthur reminds me of a baby crocodile, though he's not as good-looking, of course. Because baby crocodiles turn into big crocodiles. The longer Arthur sticks around, the more dangerous he gets. The more Gran gives him, the more he'll want. He's got a nasty appetite. At this rate, Arthur's going to ruin Gran. He'll spend all her money and her business will fall apart, and then he'll drop her. She'll end up like... like a popped balloon. Our gran, like a popped balloon in the gutter.'

'Oh, shut up, Tom. He may not be a fake, you know. Maybe he really is a spy. Maybe Lady Horsehock's fancy man is different. Or maybe Arthur's just Lady Horsehock's friend.'

'Rubbish,' said Tom decisively. 'Arthur's slippery as a slug. Slippery as an eel; a conga eel. Actually,' he added, 'he's a slippery leech. That man is a professional bloodsucker.'

'But maybe he's not,' pleaded Dan. 'Maybe, he is who he says he is and he really did have his wallet stolen.'

'Oh yeah, and maybe we're both Martians. Stop being so gullible and listen, Dan. We'll have to tell Gran.'

'But we can't,' said Dan, who hated making trouble. 'She'd be so upset. We don't know for sure that he's a crook. We can't accuse him of that

without proof.'

'Well then, we'll just have to get proof,' said Tom. 'To get to the bottom of this, we'll have to test him.'

'How?'

'Simple. We'll pretend to be some other old lady with money, and we'll go out on a date with him. Then we can grill him and trick him and we'll soon know whether he's two-timing Gran.'

'Are you mad?' gasped Dan. 'Arthur's not short-sighted like Lady Horsehock, you know. You're mad. Totally BSE-d.'

This time, Tom grabbed Dan by his two flowery collars and pulled hard.

'Listen, Dan, do you want dodgy Arthur to ruin Gran's business?'

'N-no,' stuttered Dan.

'And do you want to know the truth?'

'Y-yes.'

'Right, then,' said Tom, being very practical. 'In that case, tonight, we get Arthur's phone number and call him and arrange a date.'

'But how do we go on a date with Arthur?'

'Easy. We just pretend to be tall again. You go on my shoulders again...'

'No way, Tom. This time you go on top, because this is your idea and because I can do stage make-up and I'll need to do you up like a proper lady.'

'No, Dan. You'll be going on top. You're the one with the lovely long hair. And besides, I can't act. You can. You were complaining about missing the acting course. Well, this will make up for it. This is your big part.'

Tom gave Dan an older-brother-'I'm-so-sorry' look, and Dan knew he was beaten.

So, while Gran was in her early evening bath, Dan and Tom found her handbag and her diary.

'It's for her own good,' said Tom, opening the pink diary. 'And here's his number. Yuk, she's even drawn a heart by his name. How revolting! Right, let's call him, and you're going to do the talking because you're going to be the old lady and the voice has to be the same.'

After complaining for a bit, Dan concentrated on Tom's instructions as to what he should say. Tom found a hair-dryer and switched it on. 'This is a good sound effect. I'll blow this near the mouthpiece and it will sound to Arthur like a small plane. You can say you're in your private jet. And it'll be harder for him to hear your voice.'

'Okay, I'm ready,' said Dan, still half-wondering how Tom had talked him into this. With a shaky finger, he dialled Arthur's number. After a few rings, Arthur picked up the phone.

'Colsten Bassett 006. Good evening,' came Arthur's smooth voice down the line. Dan shot a horrified glance at Tom, but then, in his most lady-like voice, he began. 'Ah, at last. Is that Arthur Ramsbottom?'

'Yes, that's me. And who is this?'

'Oh, it's me, the Duchess of Kingsworthy. I'm ringing up about the house in the Canary Islands. Have you found me one yet?'

'I think you've got the wrong Ramsbottom,' said Arthur.

'Oh! oh, how queer,' said Dan in his poshest voice, faltering for a time, hoping that Arthur would take the bait. 'How odd. There must be two of you, then. So sorry, and it must be hard to hear me properly. I'm in my private plane and I'm afraid it is terribly noisy.'

'Yes, I can hear that. But I know how those small planes are. I've often been in them,' sympathised Arthur.

'Oh really? Well, very nice to talk to you and

I'm so sorry if I disturbed you. I'll try to find this other Arthur Ramsbottom, although I haven't been able to track him down for weeks...' The phone call was almost over. Dan wished Arthur would say goodbye.

But then Arthur took the bait. 'Maybe fate has done you a good turn,' he said. 'Because I, Arthur Ramsbottom the second, as it were – ha ha – it just so happens that I know a lot about houses in the Canary Islands. I spent a year there once, on Government business. Maybe I could be of assistance.'

'How extraordinary!' said Dan, pretending to be surprised. 'Well, well! What a coincidence! But, you know, if you could help me with my house hunt, I'd be most grateful.'

'I wouldn't do this for just anyone, Duchess,' said Arthur, 'but since you seem so – so charming, I'd be delighted to help.'

Dan couldn't believe Arthur had offered to help so quickly but he was very pleased he had, because the hair-dryer blowing near his face was making the air very hot and dry, and his voice was going croaky. 'So kind,' croaked Duchess Dan. 'Lovely. Shall we meet? We could meet for supper and talk about it. Do you like Chinese food?'

'Indeed I do. I was once on a mission in China and I grew very fond of their cuisine.'

'Well, there's a lovely Chinese restaurant called The Peking Duck. Do you know it? It's on Well Street, in Bouring-on-Sea.'

'Ah yes,' said Arthur.

'Very good. Let's meet tomorrow evening at seven o'clock, for dinner. I'll be at the back of the restaurant.'

'Sounds good to me,' agreed Arthur.

'Goodbye then, Mr Arthur Ramsbottom the second,' said Dan, simpering in his Duchess voice.

'Goodbye.'

Dan put down the phone. 'Now we've really gone and done it,' he said.

'Ramsbottom,' said Tom, 'you're rumbled.'

Chapter Eight

By six o'clock on Sunday evening, Dan and Tom were feeling very nervous. They had persuaded Gran to let them go out by themselves to see a film that was showing at the Bouring cinema, and they promised her that they'd be back by nine. 'White lies, white lies,' said Dan to Cheeky Boy. 'White Lies, white lies,' Cheeky Boy echoed back.

At six, Gran, wearing an emerald mini-skirt, popped out to see her friend Brenda for a cup of tea and a chat. 'Probably gone to tell her all about Double Agent Arthur,' said Tom.

As soon as Gran had left the flat, Tom and Dan went into her oriental bedroom. 'Cheeky boys, cheeky boys,' shouted Cheeky Boy, as they opened her wardrobe. Coloured suits and dresses hung in the cupboard.

'We'll have to choose an outfit that Arthur won't recognise,' said Tom, pulling out a leopardskin-print trouser suit. 'I know, let's wear her funeral dress. Arthur won't have seen that. It's even got a spotted veil.' Tom took out the dress and held it up to Dan. 'This would work. You'd look lovely in this, Dan.'

'Aw, shut up,' said Dan. 'You will look lovely as my bottom.'

'Thanks.'

Down in Gran's beauty parlour, Dan started to make himself up as a duchess. 'Fetch me a magazine,' he instructed Tom. 'Find me a picture of a posh old lady's face and I'll copy the make-up.'

Tom found a magazine with an advertisement for diamonds. 'You're never too old for diamonds,' read the caption under a photograph of a distinguished-looking grey-haired woman with a string of diamonds round her neck. Dan studied it. 'Right, red lipstick, lots of mascara, brown eyeshadow, pinkish cheeks, and I'll have to put my hair up. Crumbs, Tom, I'm nervous.'

'You'll be great. Just imagine you're going on the stage,' said Tom as he started to pull Dan's hair back.

'Don't you touch it,' said Dan. 'If you do it, I'll end up looking like a scarecrow.'

By six-thirty, Dan's face was looking the part. Still in his own clothes, he hurriedly left the shop with Tom. Carrying the funeral outfit in a bag, they made their way to The Peking Duck. Dan ducked and dived as they passed people in the street. He felt like a weirdo with his jeans and denim jacket on, but with a face all made-up like an old lady. He hoped that his scarf would hide his face and prayed he wouldn't bump into anyone he knew. He was very relieved when they arrived at the restaurant bang on time at six-forty.

The Peking Duck stood on the curve of Well Street. The first two letters had broken off the sign so that it read, The . . king Duck. Tom and Dan hurried inside.

'Good evening,' said the Chinese head waiter to Tom. 'Can I help?' Dan hung his head and hid his face.

'Yes,' said Tom, 'We'd like a table for two at the very back of the restaurant. Our grandmother will be joining us later with her friend.'

'So won't you be needing a table for four?'

'Er, well, no, because, you see, we will be leaving as soon as our grandmother arrives.'

'Very well.' The waiter led Tom and Dan into the restaurant.

'My grandmother would like that nice quiet table at the back. The one with the red umbrella over it would be good. She likes dark places.'

'That is not a dark place, it has low lighting,' said the waiter, slightly offended.

'Of course. It's very nice and my grandmother will like it,' said Tom.

The waiter escorted Tom and Dan to the dark table that was half hidden behind a pillar, and gave them both a menu. 'Any drinks?'

'Yes, please. Two cokes,' said Tom while Dan hid his face behind the menu. The waiter nodded and went off to deal with some other customers who'd just arrived.

'Now what?' spat Dan, who was bubbling over with nervousness. 'How am I going to get on your shoulders in here?'

'Just get up now, while the waiter's away.' Quickly Dan climbed up, but with Tom sitting, Dan's head was very high. He was going to look preposterously tall to Arthur.

Dan scrambled down. 'Yeah, Tom, I really look like a convincing old lady when I'm that size. I look like a giant. It's much better if I just kneel like this, see, that's more like the size.' Dan grabbed a cushion and put it over his heels so that kneeling wouldn't be too uncomfortable. 'Quick, give me the dress and the padding.'

Dan stuffed four pairs of old tights into one of Gran's bras which he had on and Tom put the dress over Dan's head. 'Watch my hair,' Dan whispered severely. Then he pulled the rest of the dress on, and smoothed it down. 'Do they look real?' he asked pointing to his stuffing.

'Yes, a lovely bunch of coconuts,' said Tom. 'Quick, put the veil on – the waiter'll be back soon... Wow, Dan, you really do look the part.'

'Okay, okay,' said Dan, 'Flattery won't get you anywhere. Just get under the table – the waiter's coming over with our drinks. Get under there, quick, and don't you make a sound. If you put me off, Tom, I'll kill you.'

'Okay,' said Tom diving under the table, 'and

good luck Dan. I know you're going to be brilliant.'

The waiter was walking up the restaurant with two glasses of coke. Dan smoothed down his dress and knelt up so that he looked like a convincing adult. In the dim light, his disguise was believable.

'Oh, so the boys have gone, have they?' asked the waiter. 'I didn't see them leave.'

'Yes, I'm afraid they had to go,' said Dan the Duchess. 'But I'll drink their drinks.'

'Certainly madam.' The waiter left the cokes on the table and went away again.

'I'm so nervous,' complained Dan to Tom under the table. 'This isn't like being in a play. I don't know my lines. Why did I let you talk me into doing this? I must be mad.'

'You look lovely,' said Tom, trying not to laugh. 'Just keep cool and you'll be fine.'

Dan was just about to say that he'd changed his mind and wanted to go home, when the door of the restaurant swung open and Arthur stepped inside.

Tonight, Arthur was in a light blue linen suit, a white shirt and a white tie. A spotted blue-and-white handkerchief was poked into his top pocket. The waiter gestured towards Dan's table, and Arthur, with a suave nod, started towards the table.

Arthur could see a very sombre-looking lady, sitting in the far corner of the restaurant. She appeared to be dressed for a funeral, with a veil over her face. As he drew closer, under the net he could make out fine cheekbones that blushed a delicate pink, red lips and the large nose of the woman whom he supposed was the Duchess.

'Duchess Kingsworthy?' asked Arthur in a velvety voice. 'Please don't get up. I'm Arthur Ramsbottom.'

'Oh, hello. A pleasure to meet you,' said Dan, realising that the show was now on, and that he had to play the part of the Duchess as well as he could until Arthur left and it was over. 'So,' he began, 'thank you so much for coming.' He held

out his hand and once again felt Arthur's limp handshake.

'Well,' said Arthur cosily, sitting down, 'how could I resist a call from a maiden in distress? When I heard that you needed to know about the Canary Islands, I knew I could help. But before we start talking, shall we order a drink?'

The waiter had arrived at the table again and was striking a match to light the candles on the table.

'Please, no candles,' said Dan in a panic, blowing the match out. The waiter looked surprised.

'Why ever not?' asked Arthur.

'Well, erm, I don't like fire,' said Dan the Duchess, thinking quickly. 'You see, I've been very frightened of fire, ever, er, ever since the great fire burnt down my father's castle.' Then he added, 'Luckily it was only a small one and my father had four other castles.'

'Wine?' the waiter asked.

'Ah, yes please,' said Arthur, perusing the wine list. 'Here we are – a nice bottle of Chateau Rouge, please.'

Dan gulped.

'And to eat?' the waiter asked. Quickly Dan the Duchess and Arthur looked at the menus.

'I should like sweet-and-sour pork, and spring rolls,' said Dan, as poshly as he could. 'No fish-lip soup for me!'

'Great minds think alike!' said Arthur, in a creepy, deeper voice. 'Also some won ton soup and crispy duck pancakes and some fried rice. If that's all right with you, Duchess?'

'Yes,' said Duchess Dan.

'Very good,' said the waiter. And he went away to give the cook the order.

'So,' said Arthur, turning back to the Duchess, 'You're looking for a house in the Canary Islands. Why is that?'

'Oh...' Dan hadn't thought he'd be asked questions like this. 'Because I like canaries,' he said quickly.

'How charming,' said Arthur.

'And so, where do you think I might find a very large house?' asked Duchess Dan. He thought it was best to get Arthur to do the talking.

'It really depends on how much money you have to spend,' said Arthur cautiously.

'It's only going to be a small holiday house,' said Dan, 'so I'll want to spend no more than a million.'

Arthur's Adam's apple went quietly up and down as he gulped. Then the waiter arrived with the wine. He uncorked it and poured them both a glass.

'Here's to our hunt,' said Arthur, raising his glass in a toast. Dan felt desperate as he raised his glass of wine too. As Arthur drank, Dan just touched his lips with the glass. He hoped it looked as if he was taking a sip.

'You know,' said Arthur, his eyebrows going up and down, 'it's a pity you don't like fire, because you looked very beautiful then in the match light. You're one of those rare women who has the secret of eternal youth.'

'Do you really think so?' squeaked Dan, horrified.

'Yes, I most certainly do, and I should know. On my many missions all over the world, I've only met a few women who have true beauty like yours.'

An awkward silence followed. Under the table, Tom studied Arthur's pointed crocodile-skin shoes as they curled and tapped, waiting for a reply. He felt very sorry for Dan having to eat a whole Chinese meal. Tom's stomach was lurching about from nerves but he knew his brother's would be even worse.

'That's a lovely painting, isn't it?' said Dan the Duchess, trying to change the subject and pointing to a Chinese scene on the wall behind Arthur. As Arthur turned to look at it, Dan quickly tipped his wine into a potted plant beside the table, and put some of the coke into his wine glass. In the dim light it looked like wine.

'Ah yes, a mountain scene. Very relaxing,' said Arthur.

The food arrived. Dan tried to eat as politely as possible. He was really hungry but as the Duchess he had to eat like a bird. As they nibbled their spring rolls, Arthur talked about the Canary Islands. He managed to fit in a whole lot of boasting about his job in the secret service. Dan pretended to be very interested as they ate their won ton soup. Arthur took this as encouragement and told even more stories about his adventures as a secret agent.

By the time the crispy duck pancakes arrived, Duchess Dan had been all round the world with Arthur and his wild stories. 'Of course,' said Arthur, 'you mustn't tell anyone about my past. I don't usually tell people but there's something about you that leads me to believe I can trust you.'

'Don't worry, Mr Ramsbottom. My late husband, the Duke, was in the army,' said Duchess Dan. 'He did a lot of secret work so I am used to keeping those sort of government secrets. Unfortunately though, he died in the line of duty.'

'So that's why you're wearing black?'

'Yes, in memory of him. He was a very brave man. He's been dead for two years now but I still find it difficult looking after the racehorses and all the houses, and the estates and the farms, and the yachts, not to mention the oil business.'

'So why are you buying another house in the Canaries?'

'Er, well, because I need somewhere to relax,' said Duchess Dan. 'And it'll be easy to get there in my private jet.'

By the time they'd eaten their sweet-and-sour pork and had lychees for pudding, Dan felt satisfied that Arthur was very, very impressed by the Duchess, particularly by her money. Arthur described the Canary Islands from top to bottom, and told Duchess Dan about all the nicest places there. Dan's legs were numb from kneeling. He wished the meal would end.

Under the table, Tom was drooling from all the delicious smells of Chinese food.

The bill arrived. Dan had already decided that he was definitely not paying. He had only two pounds fifty in the jeans underneath the funeral dress anyway. So, before Arthur had time to make up a hard-luck story, Duchess Dan said, 'Oh my goodness! How silly of me! I've come out without my bag!'

A tiny look of annoyance crossed Arthur's face. Then, he composed himself. 'You don't need it, dear Duchess. Dinner, of course, is on me. It's been such a pleasure to meet you.' Arthur pulled his wallet out of his inside top pocket, and removed a credit card. The waiter took the card and bill away.

'Thank you so much,' said Dan. 'What a gentleman. An exciting man like you must have so many ladies to take out.'

'Oh no,' lied Arthur. 'Actually I'm a bit of a recluse, and a loner. In my line of business I never know when duty may call. I may have to be in Japan tomorrow. So I don't have the time for lady friends. Besides, it would be difficult to know who to trust. I couldn't speak freely about my line of business, like I have with you tonight. People talk you see. No, I don't take ladies out. Haven't done so for years.'

'Oh,' said Duchess Dan, amazed by how Arthur could lie so smoothly.

'But,' continued Arthur, and here he became all syrupy again, 'but, you're the sort of woman I can trust. There's something about you that's different. Would you like to meet up again?' Arthur made a movement with his mouth as if he was mouthing the word 'prunes'. Dan felt sick, but as the Duchess he replied, 'Why yes, that would be lovely. I'll ring you tomorrow and we'll arrange a time.'

The waiter arrived with the credit card slip, and Arthur signed it. 'Thank you very much,' he said to the waiter. 'Shall we go?' he added, getting up.

'Actually, I'm going to stay a little longer,' said Dan. 'I want to talk to the waiter about China.'

'Well, it was lovely to meet you,' said Arthur. Then, to Dan's horror, when he held out his hand for Arthur to shake, Arthur seized the hand, bent down and kissed it. Arthur seemed to let his lips and moustache linger on Dan's hand. The kiss felt like a hairy tarantula with wet feet crawling over Dan's skin. Dan pulled his hand away as soon as he could.

'Goodbye,' Arthur said, making a revolting kissing shape with his lips, 'and I must say, Duchess, I look forward to hearing from you.'

'Goodbye,' said Dan, who had never been more pleased to say goodbye to anyone in his life. He watched Arthur leave the restaurant, and heaved a groan of relief. Tom popped up. 'You were brilliant,' he said with wide eyes. 'Dan, that was the best piece of acting I've ever seen – well, heard – you do. You were so convincing. You were wicked!' Tom started laughing.

'That was horrible,' said Dan. 'And my knees are killing me. I thought he'd never stop boasting and – uuurgh! Tom, you are so lucky not to have had him making eyes at you or kissing your hand.' Dan wiped his hand on a napkin. 'Uuuurgh! He is so revolting! I can't see what Gran sees in him.' Quickly, Dan peeled off his duchess clothes until he was in his jeans again. He rolled up the dress and veil and took the bra stuffing out of his shirt. Then he took some cotton wool and cream out of his pocket, and began to wipe the make-up off his face. By the time the waiter came to the table, Dan looked like a normal boy, although his cheeks were still a bit pink.

'Ah, so your grandmother has gone?'

'Yes,' said Tom, reaching in his pocket and pulling out a five pound note. 'But we'd like some crispy duck pancakes and fried rice and two more cokes, please.'

'Certainly,' said the waiter, and off he went with the order.

'I'm starving,' said Tom.

'I'm stuffed,' said Dan.

'And somehow,' said Tom, 'we've got to work out a way of making sure that Arthur gets stuffed.'

'Yes, we've got to get rid of him,' agreed Dan.

'He's a creep.'

'What a bloodsucker!'

'Poor Gran!'

'Poor Lady Horsehock.'

'Poor Duchess Kingsworthy,' said Dan.

'You mean rich Duchess Kingsworthy,' said Tom, and they both began to laugh.

Chapter Nine

'This isn't funny,' said Tom as they walked back to Gran's and talked about Arthur. 'He's got all these girlfriends and he's pretending to Gran that she's the love of his life and she's so pleased that she's blind to what he's really like. He's probably dating twenty old ladies in Bouring-on-Sea.'

'If we could look in his diary,' suggested Dan, 'we'd be able to see just how many girlfriends he's got.'

Tom shrugged, and kicked an empty can that was on the pavement. 'The thing is, Dan, we know he's lying to Gran, and that's enough. All this secret service stuff is such rubbish. The guy's a wimp. He couldn't defend himself if a sausage dog attacked him.'

'Actually Tom, we don't know that for sure. He definitely does have lots of girlfriends, but I still think maybe he really is in the secret service. I mean James Bond always has lots of girlfriends doesn't he? And he's still 007.'

'James Bond is big and muscly and cool. Dodgy Arthur is skinny, weak and creepy, and so obviously not in the secret service, Dan.'

'Maybe in real life people in the secret service don't look all muscly like James Bond. Have you thought about that? Maybe they all look creepy like Arthur. I saw a really weak-looking karate teacher once.'

'Bet he was more muscly than Arthur,' said Tom. 'Anyway, this isn't really the most important thing here. The fact is, he is definitely not being honest with Gran and we've got to tell her.'

'How? I'm not telling,' said Dan, who hated the idea of upsetting Gran.

Tom thought for a moment. Visions of Gran bursting into tears, of Cheeky Boy saying 'Nasty boy, nasty boy,' and then of Gran sending Tom packing, filled his mind. 'She wouldn't believe us,' he said.

As they walked up the hill towards Gran's house, Tom was lost in thought. Dan knew not to interrupt him. He knew Tom would come up with a solution soon, but he made up his mind that if Tom's new plan had anything to do with getting him to act again, he was going to refuse.

Finally, at the top of the hill, Tom stopped. 'I've got it,' he said. 'We show Arthur up in front of Gran, and while we're at it, in front of Lady Horsehock too.'

'How do we do that?'

'Simple. We put him in a situation where he has to act like a secret agent, and if he doesn't, well then, they'll both see he's a fake.'

'That doesn't sound simple at all to me,' Dan said suspiciously.

'Imagine this: Arthur, Gran, and Lady H are all in one place, and suddenly the door opens and in comes a really scary man with a stocking over his head. He barges in holding a gun – an automatic machine-gun, and he points the gun at them all, and he demands their money or their lives. You know, like a highwayman.'

'Tom, they don't say that any more. They say: 'Freeze, this is a hold up, and if you want to see tomorrow, lady, you'd better do as I say!'

'Exactly Dan. You've got it already. You're a natural. You're going to be brilliant.'

'No way, Tom, I'm not doing it. No way. First of all, my head is too small, and I'm not muscly enough. They'd all see it was me on your shoulders.'

'Nah, nah, nah,' said Tom. 'This time, I'll do the body really professionally, and I'll make you look like a real thug.'

'Listen, Tom! If I do look real, what if Arthur really can do aikido and what if he does a death blow on me, or on you? What if he does a judo kick and knocks you out, Tom?'

'Aw, wake up, Dan, he's not for real. That guy couldn't kick a football.'

'But what if Lady Horsehock has a heart attack?'

'Now you really are scraping the barrel for excuses,' said Tom, rubbing his nose on his shoulder like a boxer who'd won a fight.

'But where would we do it?' said Dan, desperate for a reason not to do it.

'At Marjorie's Tea House of course. We'll pull Marjorie in on the act. She'll love it. This is it, Dan. We've got to finish what we started. We've got to do it.'

Marjorie's Tea House was a rickety old café up a little side street near the waterfront in Bouring. Marjorie herself was a slightly dotty old friend of Gran's and had known the boys since they were babies. Marjorie was very eccentric she was enormously fat and often wore very strange flowing clothes. Sometimes she sang in her tea rooms to the captive audience who'd come for tea. You see, Marjorie loved the theatre and took part in the Bouring Amateur Dramatic group plays as often as she could. Most years, Tom and Dan visited Marjorie, so Marjorie was due a visit. She always loved to see the boys.

Back at Gran's that evening, Tom telephoned Marjorie.

'Oh, Tommy, Tommy-boy, you're here! And Danny, Danny-boy too! Why haven't you two visited? I heard about your mother going to America and I think it's shocking that you two had to miss your summer theatre club. Just shocking! Grown-ups can be so selfish sometimes!' Marjorie was obviously very much on Tom and Dan's side, which was good. So Tom began to tell her all about what had happened, about how Arthur was using Gran, about how Gran's business was in danger, about how they'd had to dress up as Gran, about how they'd pretended to be rich Duchess Kingsworthy, and how they'd found out Arthur would go out with anyone who had a bit of money. Lastly, Tom told Marjorie how Arthur made everyone think he was a spy, but that he was a fake.

'But,' shouted Dan, trying to grab the phone, 'we don't know he's a fake for sure.'

Marjorie was amazed. Tom went on to tell her about their plan to catch Dodgy Arthur out. 'I know it's a lot to ask, Marjorie, but if you could help us by letting a robbery happen in your tea house, and, if you could act – you know – that you're really frightened too, then I think the plan will work.'

'Oooh, Tom,' said Marjorie indulgently. 'You are a little tyke. Quite devious. But I can see your problem, and I do like your gran, and it sounds to me as though this Arthur needs to be put to the test. What's more, you know I've got a soft spot for acting. So, Tom – for you, Dan, your gran, and for me – I'll do it.'

'Fantastic!' said Tom. 'You're a gem, Marje. When shall we do it then?'

'Thursday afternoons are always quiet,' said Marjorie. 'That would be the perfect time. Why don't I invite your gran over for 3.30 on Thursday afternoon. I know she'll arrive five minutes early.' Marjorie was really getting into the swing of things.

'And we'll get Lady Horsehock down there, and Arthur of course, at 3.30 too,' said Tom.

'If you arrive at about 1.30, we can have rehearsals,' said Marjorie excitedly.

'It will be nice to work with you,' said Tom. 'Goodbye, Marjorie and see you Thursday.'

'Goodbye, Tom, and tell Dan how excited I am.'

Marjorie hung up. 'That's set then,' said Tom. 'We'll write an invitation for Lady Horsehock, and you can telephone Arthur pretending to be Duchess Kingsworthy again, and invite him to tea on Thursday. I'll sort out the costume. It's going to be fairly tricky.'

'Piece of cake, piece of cake,' sang Cheeky Boy, flapping over and hopping onto Dan's shoulder. Dan fed Cheeky Boy another nut. At least, he supposed, this would be the final act. Anyway, he had always fancied playing a hood.

Chapter Ten

On Monday Tom and Dan typed an invitation for Lady Horsehock. Tom signed the invitation 'Arthur' using Gran's fountain pen. He thought the handwriting looked exactly like Arthur's would. After posting the letter, he and Dan felt sure that Lady Horsehock would turn up. She probably did nothing on Thursday afternoons.

Dan then made the dreaded call to Arthur, as Duchess Kingsworthy. 'So, would you care to meet me at Marjorie's Tea House, for tea?' Dan the Duchess asked.

'That would be an incredible pleasure for me,' said dodgy Arthur. 'It will be lovely to see you in the light of day. I have such memories of your beautiful face.'

Dan struggled to carry on in his posh-lady voice. 'Oh well, I'm so pleased. See you on Thursday, then,' and he put the phone down. 'Uuurgh! I'm going to be sick,' he said. 'He is so creepy!'

Tom had a good laugh when Dan repeated Arthur's side of the conversation.

The rest of the week was a challenge for Tom as he looked for ways to build up Dan's body under a long coat which they bought from a charity shop for three pounds. Tom made a set of muscles from scraps of material, and glued and sewed them all down the chest and arms of one of Dan's long-sleeved tee shirts. He built up the shoulders on the tee shirt so that they were broad like a wrestler's. With the long black coat over the top, Dan appeared to have the body of a body-builder but he still had the neck of a scrawny chicken. So Tom made a special neck-piece, which, if worn with a scarf over it, gave Dan a big, fat muscly neck. Lastly, Tom built a papier mâché face, with foam padding, for Dan to wear over his own. With a stocking pulled over the top, it looked very realistic.

By Wednesday afternoon the costume was almost finished. 'Wicked, Dan, you look bad,' said Tom gleefully. Tom found himself a pair of men's shoes in the charity shop, and on Wednesday night he pleaded with Dan not to eat too much until the ordeal was over. Dan was heavy enough without a big meal inside him.

Gran, meanwhile, went for quite a few spins in Arthur's car, and bought him lots more presents. More worryingly, she cancelled some of her mid-week appointments.

On Thursday morning Dan woke up with butterflies in his stomach, which grew more and more fluttery as the day went on. At last, after lunch, the wait was over, and the two brothers made their way down to the Bouring waterfront, to Marjorie's Tea House, carrying their disguise in three plastic bags.

'Lovely to see you,' shrieked Marjorie, flinging the door open and appearing in a dress that looked like a blue tent. 'And I'm so looking forward to the show,' she said, turning a sign in the door so that it read 'Out for lunch'.

Marjorie had grown even fatter since the year before, which wasn't surprising as she lived off a diet of cakes and scones. Sometimes she'd eat a Marmite sandwich, but that was about as savoury as she got. She never ate vegetables and she thought that eating salad was like eating grass. It always surprised Tom and Dan that she managed to stay alive eating the rubbish that she did, but survive she did, and she was very nice and very jolly with it. Always in a good mood and always ready for a laugh.

Tom and Dan followed her massive form into the back room where they'd spent many happy hours watching old movies on video.

'This is going to be so much fun!' said Marjorie, opening a bag of toffees and offering it to the boys. She took three for herself, unwrapped them and popped them all at once into her red lipsticked mouth.

'I need energy for the rehearsal,' she explained chewing. 'I wish you'd told me earlier about all of this. I could have hired a real gun and then we could've really scared this Arthur when you fired it at the ceiling. I wouldn't mind a hole in the ceiling of the tea house – no one ever looks up. They're always looking down at their cakes.'

'That might have been a bit dangerous,' said Dan.

'Dangerous, but fun,' said Marjorie. 'You only live once.'

Aaaaah

Tom looked at Dan, and smiled. Marjorie was perfect. She was slightly mad but very game.

'We thought,' said Tom, 'that we'd use this gun we've made, and hide it under a bit of material. See?' Tom pulled the fake gun from under the material and pointed it at Marjorie.

'Aaaaaah,' Marjorie screamed, walking

backwards into the TV and nearly knocking it over.

'No, it's not real Marjorie, it's a fake! Tom made it,' said Dan, trying to calm her down.

'Oooh, you two, oh my goodness, you nearly gave me a heart attack there.' Dan gulped. He hoped Lady Horsehock wouldn't have a heart attack when 3.30 came.

After an hour and a quarter's rehearsing with Marjorie, Tom and Dan started to feel excited about the afternoon's performance. They went into Marjorie's back room, and there they waited. The back room had a door out onto the side street, so that once Arthur, Lady Horsehock and Gran were all in the tea room, Dan and Tom could go out onto the street, round the corner and in through the door of the Tea House.

At three twenty Lady Horsehock arrived. Tom and Dan watched through Marjorie's secret spyhole. Lady Horsehock still had a stain around the top of her head, and hardly any eyebrows, although her hair looked tidier than it had done on Saturday. Wearing a mink coat, she was guided by Marjorie to a window table. Dan managed to lipread as Lady Horsehock said, 'I'm here to meet an Arthur Ramsbottom', and 'a pot of tea please.'

At three twenty-five, Gran arrived. Compared with the dull colours of Lady Horsehock's brown tweed suit, Gran's outfit was very colourful – a purple zebraskin-patterned dress, a pair of pink stilettos and a blue-and-green flowery coat. Gran soon spotted Lady Horsehock at the window table. Tom and Dan couldn't hear what the two ladies were saying but they seemed quite pleased to see one another.

'Hello, Lady Horsehock,' Gran was saying. 'Nice to see you here. Are you on your own?' Gran looked at Lady Horsehock's hair and eyebrows and wondered what had happened.

'No, no, dear, I'm meeting someone,' said Lady Horsehock importantly, the pearls round her neck gleaming in the afternoon light.

'Lovely. Well don't let me barge in. See you soon, I hope,' said Gran before finding Marjorie behind the till. She went over to say hello to her.

'Hannah – so glad you could come!' said Marjorie. 'Why don't you sit here while I make this lady's tea, then I'll sit down too and have a chat.' Marjorie sat Gran at a table near the wall, carefully placed so that she had a restricted view of the tea rooms, and no view at all of the door.

Finally, at three thirty precisely, Arthur arrived, very pleased that he was about to have tea with the Duchess Kingsworthy. He took off his trilby hat and his lightweight Ulster coat, revealing green tweed plus fours, green knee-length socks, a green tweed jacket, a white shirt and a brown tie. Marjorie asked him if he had booked a table. 'My name's Arthur Ramsbottom.' he said quietly, 'and – '

But before Arthur could finish his sentence, Marjorie quickly said, 'Ah yes, over here,' and led him to Lady Horsehock's table.

'Hello Arthur, so nice to see you,' said Lady Horsehock, who could just make out the blur that was Arthur.

As Arthur scanned the tea rooms for Duchess Kingsworthy, to his horror he saw Gran instead, reading a magazine at a table by the wall. Arthur put his hand up to his face to try and conceal his identity.

'Are you all right Mr Ramsbottom?' Marjorie asked him. 'Have you got toothache?'

'No, everything's fine,' said Arthur quietly, sitting down opposite Lady Horsehock and trying to compose himself. This was a tricky situation. He'd been in trouble like this before with other ladies. He knew it was his own fault for going out with so many at once, but that didn't make this predicament any easier. He hoped that both these ladies remembered his 'Emergency Procedure'.

As Lady Horsehock asked him what he'd like for tea, Arthur glanced up again, towards the back of the café to see if Gran had seen him. And at that moment, too, Gran looked up. An expression of surprise and joy crossed her face, but before she'd had time to voice her pleasure, Arthur put a finger to his lips as if to say 'shhhh'.

Gran, thinking that this was a sign that he was

doing some secret service work, didn't say a word. As she twisted her napkin, she wondered why Arthur should be spying on Lady Horsehock. Maybe Lady Horsehock wasn't as innocent as she looked.

So there was the situation: Lady Horsehock having tea with Arthur, and Arthur pretending to Gran that he was on a secret mission, and Gran thinking that she must pretend not to know him.

Marjorie brought cakes and everyone began drinking tea. Of course, the main thought in Arthur's head was that Duchess Kingsworthy might turn up any second. Arthur leant over to old Lady Horsehock and confidentially told her that in a minute he might have to get up and talk to a strange woman. 'Is it a mission, Arthur?' asked Lady Horsehock, her huge eyes blinking widely behind her thick spectacles.

'Yes, Daphne. A mission. So, I'm going to move to another table, and when this lady arrives, you must sit here quietly and ignore me.'

'Marvellous! Gosh, this is exciting!' exclaimed Lady Horsehock, in a whisper.

Gran was very excited too. Both ladies were thrilled to be seeing Arthur on duty at last. Arthur got up and moved to another table.

Marjorie sensed the moment was right. She walked towards the secret spyhole and winked at Tom and Dan. This was it.

Dan, already wearing the muscle outfit and the mask, put the coat on. He climbed onto Tom's shoulders and checked in the mirror that the coat was covering both of them. They looked very convincing. Then he pulled the fake gun, covered in a big black scarf, out of his pocket, and Tom walked towards the door. Tom stepped out into the alley and walked around to the front of the Tea House. The street was quiet. There they stood, an armed robber on the corner of the street...

'Ready, Dan?' came Tom's muffled voice from under the coat.

'Ready,' said Dan, in character, in a deep aggressive voice. Then he added, in a nervous tremolo, 'But, whatever you do, Tom, don't fall over... And, if he does attack...'

'Just get on with it, Dan,' Tom said. 'What are you, a man or a mouse?'

'Neither,' said Dan, 'but let's go.' Tom pushed open the door, and stepped inside.

Dan slammed the tea room door behind him and seized Marjorie. Pointing the gun at her, he shouted in a deep American voice, 'Okay, lady, this is a hold-up, and if you know what's good for you, you'll co-operate, or this could get nasty.'

Marjorie screamed and looked terrified. She shied away from Dan but he roughly held her arm. Lady Horsehock squinted up at the entrance to the Tea House. 'Did somebody just come in?' she asked

Arthur. Gran held her teacup frozen in mid-air, terrified. Arthur sat in his chair, looking up, still as a statue. Dan turned the gun on the three of them.

Gran made a squeaky, yelping sound. Lady Horsehock croaked, 'Is he holding a gun?' but Arthur still didn't make a move.

From underneath the overcoat, Tom wished he could see more of what was going on. As it was, he was in woolly darkness and he could hardly breathe.

He wondered what Arthur was doing. His conviction that Arthur was a fraud was draining away from him. Maybe Arthur really was an agent. Maybe he really was a black belt aikido. Tom braced himself and then Dan's leg dug into his right side, indicating that he wanted to go right. Tom felt like a scared donkey.

'Shut up you two!' Dan ordered the women. 'And you, Mister. If you want to walk out of here alive, you'll co-operate too. Now put your hands in the air.'

All the tea-drinkers put their hands in the air, and Marjorie made some more distressed noises. 'Please don't hurt me!' she pleaded. 'What do you want? If it's money you want, I'll open the till.'

'Yes, if it's money that you want,' shouted Lady Horsehock bravely, 'I've got stables full. Just ask, you don't have to frighten the poor woman.'

'Yes,' agreed Gran, taking her necklace off. 'You can have all my jewellery too.'

'Shut it, you two,' growled Dan, now in full flow. 'Throw your bags on the floor. You too.' Dan pointed the gun at Arthur... 'I said you, too, Mister. You throw your wallet.'

Gran and Lady Horsehock did as they were told. Dan's gun hovered in mid-air, pointing at Arthur. Arthur was sitting bolt upright. Surprisingly quiet. Dangerously still. A wave of fear flooded through Dan. What if Arthur had a real gun! He had a defiant look in his eyes, as if he was about to make a move.

'I told you, Mister!' Dan spat, as fiercely as he could, 'Throw your wallet on the floor, or you're history.'

Granny Hannah and Lady Horsehock looked at Arthur lovingly. Of course, poor Arthur had had his wallet stolen. But then, to their surprise, Arthur reached into his top inside pocket and pulled out his old familiar crocodile wallet and threw it on the floor.

'Good, good,' said Dan, with the gun, forcing Marjorie to pick up the wallet and the bags. Then, walking backwards towards the cash desk with Marjorie, Dan indicated with the gun that he wanted her to empty the till. Marjorie, acting brilliantly, shaking and nodding, obeyed. 'Now,' Dan said, 'get on the floor, all of you.'

Gran hitched up her dress and knelt on the floor and helped Lady Horsehock down. There they both lay on their stomachs. Marjorie lowered herself with difficulty and finally, Arthur lay on the floor too.

Gran looked at Arthur with sparkling wide eyes. She was nervous, but with Arthur around she felt sure that he'd suddenly take control of the situation, and everything would be all right. After all, Arthur had been in a thousand dangerous situations like this. This was nothing to him. He'd been in conditions a hundred times worse. As the man with the stocking over his face was emptying the till Gran couldn't help leaning over to Arthur and saying, 'Remember, Arthur, how you fought off that pack of eleven, in the jungle in Africa, when you were unarmed, and they all had machine-guns?'

Arthur nodded at Gran but put his finger to his lips, warning her to stay quiet.

Then, to Gran's surprise, Lady Horsehock said quietly, 'Yes, Arthur, you show him. Move in on him now, while he's counting the money. Use your aikido.'

Arthur looked at Lady Horsehock and nodded. Gran thought this was a licence to whisper. 'What are you going to do, Arthur? Why don't you get him in an arm lock?'

'Yes, give him a good karate chop where it hurts,' suggested Lady Horsehock, 'and then hit him over the head with the till.' Lady Horsehock was enjoying the idea of a fight; a strange, violent expression had crossed her face.

'Well, don't be too nasty,' said Gran, who didn't

like the sight of blood.

'No, don't be too nasty,' whispered Marjorie, worried suddenly that Arthur might actually try to do something.

'But whatever you do, do it now,' said Lady Horsehock bossily. 'Or he'll get away.'

At last Arthur got to his feet, in a crouching way. Dan could see him out of the corner of his eye. Arthur's movements behind him filled Dan with alarm. If Arthur was about to spring on him and karate chop him into a thousand pieces, Dan was not looking forward to it.

Arthur got up and took a step forwards. Lady Horsehock and Gran were proud to see him in action. Marjorie was ready to spring up and restrain him.

Arthur took another step forwards, about to attack. Dan braced himself.

But then, with a movement like a slippery eel, Arthur grabbed the handle of the Tea House door, opened it, and in a second, he was out. Out, half walking, half running, down the street and away from the Tea House. His green tweed suit disappeared around a corner.

Dan whispered into his coat, 'He's scarpered.'

'Yes-s-s!' came Tom's whispered reply. But the show wasn't quite over yet. The two boys turned round.

'Where's the man gone?' Dan the thug grunted.

'He's run off,' said Marjorie. Gran, now petrified, kept her eyes tightly shut. Dan gathered up the money from the till, the handbags and from Arthur's wallet, and said, 'Right, I'm off and you ladies'd better keep your traps shut and not call the police for twenty minutes or I'll be back to get you.'

'All right,' said Marjorie. 'We won't.'

And with that, Tom carried Dan out of the Tea House. They walked round to the side alley and into the back of Marjorie's house. They collapsed on the sofa. Tom threw Dan off his shoulders. 'It worked!' he laughed, red in the face. 'I can't believe it. It worked!'

Dan was still stunned from the performance he'd just given. 'I deserve an Oscar!' he declared.

In the Tea House, the three ladies peeled themselves off the floor. They were all very shaken (even though Marjorie was only pretending).

'What a horrid experience,' said Gran, sitting in a chair, wondering where Arthur had gone.

'That was ghastly,' complained Lady Horsehock. 'What is the world coming to?' Both sat breathing heavily, both wondering whether the robbery had been something to do with the secret service.

Finally, when they had caught their breath, Gran turned to Lady Horsehock, and said, 'So, I didn't know you knew Arthur.'

'Oh yes,' said Lady Horsehock, 'Well we've been dating, you see. How do you know him? Is he an old friend?'

'No,' said Gran, with her mouth open. 'I've been dating him too.'

Now it was Lady Horsehock's turn to stare open-mouthed. 'But...' she spluttered, 'he said I was the only woman in his life.'

'He said he loved me,' squeaked Gran.

There was a long silence, as the feelings of both ladies turned from hurt to humiliation to anger.

'Why, that two-timing, double-crossing slime ball,' exploded Gran furiously. 'How could he? How dare he? I haven't been two-timed since I was sixteen! I can't believe I didn't see through him! Why, I'll – I'll tie him to my massage table and slowly pluck out that horrid little moustache of his!'

Then it was Lady Horsehock's turn to go mad. 'I've never been so humiliated,' she snarled. 'That man's a rat. After all I did for him. I'll set my bally hounds on him. They'll chase him across the countryside and they'll tear him apart, and they'll gobble him up, and he'll deserve it!'

Both women fumed as they thought of double-dealing Arthur.

'And,' said Hannah, 'how could he have left us all here with that horrible masked thug, and run off like he did? The man has no standards.'

'It's shocking,' agreed Lady Horsehock. 'After all the years he's been working for the secret service, you'd think he might stick his scrawny neck out for us.' Her voice quaked again. 'In fact, I'd like to take his yellow cravat and wring that scrawny neck of his.' Lady Horsehock had a bloodthirsty look in her eye.

'I suppose he may,' reasoned Gran, 'have been on a mission, but a gentleman agent would have looked after the ladies. I'd like to smother that fancy car of his with nail polish.'

'I'd like to run him over with my Bentley,' insisted Lady Horsehock.

Marjorie then spoke up. 'I'm sorry to suggest this, girls, but hasn't it crossed your minds that a man who's been dishonest with you about who he loves, might also have been dishonest about what he does?'

'What? D'you think that he mightn't be in the secret service after all?' exclaimed Gran.

'Do you think he's a fraud?' choked Lady Horsehock.

And all at once the big fat penny dropped.

Chapter Eleven

After Lady Horsehock and Gran had gone home, Marjorie came out the back to congratulate the boys.

'You were marvellous,' she said, 'so professional. Hollywood, look out! You, Dan, should star in movies, and you, Tom – you've got a career in special effects.'

'We couldn't have done it without you,' said Dan. 'You being scared really persuaded them that it was real. And I can't believe what a crumby coward that dodgy Arthur is.'

'I can,' said Tom.

'Wonder where he ran to,' said Dan.

'Well, he probably went to the address that's on the driving licence in his wallet. We're posting his wallet and his coat and hat back. Your gran and Lady H are writing him letters saying how disgusting he is. Oh, and by the way, I told them that I'd report the robbery to the police, which I won't, of course.'

'What shall we do with all the money from the robbery? There was ten pounds in Arthur's wallet, fifty pounds in Lady Horsehock's bag and twenty pounds in Gran's,' said Tom.

'I think,' said Marjorie, 'you boys should take Arthur's money as wages. It was only ten pounds. You've earned it. But we must give your gran and

Lady Horsehock's money back, even though you've saved both those ladies a lot of heartache.'

Marjorie gave both the boys a hug, and at five thirty, they left the Tea House.

Back at Gran's the atmosphere was gloomy. She was nursing a broken heart. Cheeky Boy, picking up on her mood, sang, 'Poor Hannah, poor Hannah, poor Hannah.' Of course, Gran told the boys about everything and they pretended to be amazed. Then they helped her feel better by telling her how wonderful she was and what a shmuck Arthur was. They explained how she was lucky to be rid of him. Gran agreed with them and cheered up a little.

By Saturday, Gran was back to her cheerful self. To lift her spirits, Dan let her cut his hair; his fringe at least.

'Now you'll be able to see,' said Gran, as she swept up the floor.

'Mmmmm,' agreed Tom quietly. 'And next time we come across a liar, you won't be so gullible.'

Then, on Saturday afternoon, their mum's small blue car drew up outside Hannah's Heaven.

Tom and Dan heard her shouting up at the window of their bedroom. 'Yooo hooo, Tom, Dan!'

They both looked out of the window to see

their dad standing on the street with a strange woman. She had big puffy lips, two black eyes, a small nose and very big you-know-whats.

Tom and Dan rushed downstairs. Gran was already on the street talking to their dad and the woman.

'Mum?' said Dan. 'Hi Dad. Is that you, Mum? Are you all right? Your eyes are all bruised, and your nose...'

'Is that really you, Mum?' said Tom. 'Hi Dad.'

Mr Bugsby had a big smile on his face, as if to say 'It's a surprise, isn't it?'

'Ooooh haven't they done a lovely job,' sighed Gran, appreciatively. 'I told you those plastic surgeons in America were good, didn't I, love?'

Tom and Dan's mum hugged them both, which was a strange experience as it felt as though she had two water-filled balloons under her shirt.

'But Mum,' said Dan, 'you said it was Aunty Saz who was having the plastic surgery.'

'That's because I didn't want you to worry about me,' said their mum.

Tom and Dan were speechless for a second. Then Tom turned to Dan, and talking slowly like a wise and ancient Chinese philosopher, said to him, 'But Dan, have you not learnt yet... Things are not always as they seem.'